Mary Had a Great Big Dog

♫ Sing to the tune of "Mary Had a Little Lamb."

By Maria Fleming

Mary had a great big dog,
great big dog, great big dog.

Mary had a great big dog.
She brought him to the fair.

Freddy had a bigger dog,
bigger dog, bigger dog.

Freddy had a bigger dog,
bigger than a bear!

Becky had the biggest dog,
biggest dog, biggest dog.

Becky had the biggest dog,

the very biggest there!